10/18

A.R. 3.5

Maddy McGuire, CEO

Crafting For A Cause

Calico

An Imprint of Magic Wagon
abdopublishing.com

By Emma Bland Smith Illustrated by Lissy Marlin

For my nephew and niece, Carver and Aija Beitiks, who
make the holidays extra special–EBS

To my lucky stars, thanks for lighting my way–LM

abdopublishing.com

Published by Magic Wagon, a division of ABDO, PO Box 398166,
Minneapolis, Minnesota 55439. Copyright © 2019 by Abdo
Consulting Group, Inc. International copyrights reserved in all
countries. No part of this book may be reproduced in any form
without written permission from the publisher. Calico™ is a
trademark and logo of Magic Wagon.

Printed in the United States of America, North Mankato,
Minnesota.
052018
092018

Written by Emma Bland Smith
Illustrated by Lissy Marlin
Edited by Bridget O'Brien
Art Directed by Laura Mitchell

Library of Congress Control Number: 2018931815

Publisher's Cataloging-in-Publication Data

Names: Smith, Emma Bland, author. | Marlin, Lissy, illustrator.
Title: Crafting for a cause / by Emma Bland Smith; illustrated by Lissy Marlin.
Description: Minneapolis, Minnesota ; Magic Wagon, 2019. | Series: Maddy McGuire, CEO
Summary: Maddy and Darcy can't wait to begin their new gift-wrapping business to buy
    presents for the grown-ups at their school. They invite Maddy's new neighbor, Amina,
    to join them. Amina is from Syria. She had to leave her grandparents behind, but is
    excited to experience life in America and be part of a group. The girls busy
    themselves with crafts and learning about social media. When they finally open their
    business, Maddy changes her mind about who to give the money to. There's just one
    problem. What Amina needs most isn't something you can raise money for.
Identifiers: ISBN 9781532131844 (lib.bdg.) | ISBN 9781532132247 (ebook) |
    ISBN 9781532132445 (Read-to-me ebook)
Subjects: LCSH: Handicraft--Juvenile fiction. | Extended families--Juvenile fiction. |
    Social media--Juvenile fiction. | Friendship--Juvenile fiction.
Classification: DDC [E]--dc23

TABLE OF CONTENTS

Chapter One

Whoosh! A gust of wind sent wrapping paper and ribbons flying across the room. Maddy jumped up and slammed the window shut.

She'd opened it that morning to say hi to Darcy. She had forgotten to close it. Even in Northern California, late December meant blustery weather.

Her bedroom door had a gap on the bottom. It was letting in a delicious smell. Maddy sniffed. Brown sugar and butter!

That meant Mom was making lace cookies, her favorite! Maddy sighed with contentment as she tied the ribbon on her brother's present.

Maddy had made her family's gifts. A rose petal sachet for Mom. A painted rock for Dad. And for Drew, a picture of his new pet fish in a frame.

She opened her desk drawer to grab the sachet. She glanced at her class photo on top of a pile of papers. Her teacher smiled at her.

An arrow of panic pinged Maddy. She had to get a present for Ms. Wilson! Maddy wrapped the sachet, her mind racing.

What about the secretaries? And the librarian? And the garden teacher? And the crossing guard? Her school had so many awesome grown-ups!

Her family liked her homemade gifts. But she felt a little silly giving the teachers and adults at school painted rocks.

They deserved nice gifts. Like earrings for Ms. Wilson. And seedlings for the garden teacher. And a book for Ms. Katey, the librarian.

But those things were expensive. She was going to need money. Again.

Maddy thought about the businesses she'd had in the past. Last summer, she'd run a day camp. It paid for horseback riding lessons.

She and Darcy created an outdoor movie theater just before Halloween. It paid for the annual block party permit.

What could she do to raise money to buy holiday gifts? She and Darcy would have to brainstorm soon.

"Darn," she said aloud, starting on Dad's present. How did she go through all that tape already? She headed down the stairs.

Just as she grabbed the tape from the dresser in the hall, two things happened. The kitchen timer dinged (lace cookies!) and the doorbell rang.

The oven door clanged as Mom pulled out the cookies. Then Mom dashed into the hall.

"Oh good, Mads, you're here!" Mom said. "Can you take the cookies off the baking sheet? I need to get the door."

"Sure." As Maddy transferred the cookies to a rack, she listened. Mom was talking with someone at the front door.

"From Syria? Oh my goodness!" she heard Mom say.

"They've been in a transition home for a few months," said a voice. Maddy recognized it as Meredith's, a neighbor across the street. "They're living with us until their home is ready."

Maddy heard more snippets. "War," "refugee," "escape." She shivered, despite the heat from the oven.

The conversation went on. Mom loved to chat. It was one of the many differences between her and Maddy. Then she heard Mom say her name.

"My daughter Maddy is nine. How old are you?"

"I'm nine, too," said a new voice. A younger one.

Maddy paused, spatula mid-air. She knew what was coming.

"Let me introduce you," Mom said.

Maddy felt a pit in her stomach.

It wasn't that she was unfriendly. It just took Maddy a while to feel comfortable around new people. Grown-ups assumed that because you're the same age as someone, you'd be best friends.

Sure enough, Mom came into the kitchen with a girl. She had soft brown skin, big brown eyes, and dark hair. She wore jeans and a hoodie.

"Maddy, this is Amina," said Mom. "She's from Syria. She's staying with the Wolf family for a while."

"Hi! Nice to meet you!" said Amina.

Maddy was surprised that Amina spoke such good English. She had just a bit of an accent, musical and pretty.

"Hi," Maddy said back. Amina's smile was so big that Maddy couldn't help returning it.

"Why don't you bring her to your room?" said Mom. She was heading back to the door. Meredith and Amina's mom stood there talking.

Maddy nodded and headed for the stairs. She looked over her shoulder to encourage Amina to follow her.

Maddy thought of the snippets she'd overheard. Especially the word "war." She wondered what it would feel like to have to be forced to leave your home.

She thought of the biggest problem *she'd* faced all day. No more tape. Her face felt warm.

Chapter Two

As they passed the living room, Amina paused. "So pretty!" she said, and Maddy followed her gaze. The Christmas tree twinkled with fancy and homemade ornaments.

Nutcrackers stood on the mantel. Paper snowflakes festooned the windows. A garland hung over the doorway. Red and green pillows decorated the sofa.

Just the sight gave Maddy a cozy, warm feeling. Did it do the same for Amina?

"Thank you," said Maddy. "Did you have a Christmas tree? In Syria?"

They started up the stairs. Amina shook her head. "Oh no," she said. "We don't celebrate Christmas."

Maddy knew not everyone celebrated Christmas. Lots of people at her school celebrated Hanukkah and Kwanzaa. At the winter concert, the students sang carols from lots of different cultures.

"Are you . . . Jewish?" Once more, her cheeks burned and she felt silly.

Amina shook her head again. But she smiled, and Maddy relaxed a little. "I'm Muslim. It's a religion. Most people in Syria are Muslim."

"Oh, right," said Maddy. She knew several Muslim families from school.

Maddy opened her door. She wondered if Amina's holiday traditions included giant wrapping paper messes.

In her room, ribbon and paper covered her desk. Maddy's wrapped gifts lay in the middle.

"Oh, I love presents!" said Amina.

Maddy smiled. "I know, so do I! I love giving them more than getting them!"

"Me too!" said Amina. "Well, almost." They both giggled.

"This year I'm giving presents to some grown-ups at school." Maddy explained she was still thinking of a way to raise the money. Then she asked, "Do you give presents in Syria?"

Amina tilted her head. "Sometimes we give birthday presents. We also have a holiday called Eid al-Fitr. You could say it's sort of our Christmas.

"On Eid, we wear new clothes. Everyone is nice and happy and we eat yummy things. The grown-ups give kids presents. And we help people in need. It's the best day of the year!"

Amina made a funny happy face and hugged herself. Maddy laughed.

As it turned out, a love for holidays wasn't the only thing the girls had in common. Over the next hour, Amina and Maddy cut, colored, and glittered.

Amina asked one question after another about life in America. Especially school.

Her mother was going to the school district tomorrow. She was going to ask about enrolling Amina. Amina wanted to know everything!

Maddy was explaining how to play kickball when Mom opened the door. She looked up from cutting out a miniature gingerbread cookie.

"I come bearing cookies." Mom held out a plate. "How's everything going?"

Amina smiled. "Maddy has the most lovely art supplies," she said.

Mom sat on the small armchair by the door. "Her grandfather is an artist. He always gives Maddy new art supplies for birthdays and Christmas."

"That's nice," said Amina. "I wish my grandparents were here. But they weren't able to come with us." She looked back at her paper, and continued sprinkling glitter.

Amina's eyes crinkled, just a bit. Maddy knew that feeling, the one that came before tears.

Mom knew it, too. She stood and set the plate on the desk. "I'm off. Amina, have you ever had Christmas cookies? It's one of our favorite traditions."

Amina's face relaxed and she reached for a lace cookie. "Oh, I could eat ten hundred of these!"

"Bye, girls, have fun crafting. Feel free to wrap my presents when you're done, Maddy!" Mom gave a laugh and shut the door behind her.

The girls munched on cookies. They examined the colorful mess on the floor.

"Maybe I'll make a card to send to my grandparents," said Amina. She began to rummage in the scrap paper box.

Maddy gathered up her courage. "Why didn't your grandparents come with you?" she asked.

Amina paused before answering. "We didn't have enough money."

Maddy started a snowflake. "That's happened to me. Last year I wanted to take horseback riding lessons . . ."

Maddy's voice faded. How could she compare lessons to getting your grandparents out of a war zone? Would Amina think she was spoiled?

But Amina just nodded sympathetically. And then she asked

another question about school in America.

Maddy snipped her snowflake. It occurred to her that Amina was probably going to be at her school. Maybe she'd even be in Ms. Wilson's class, too!

Maddy snipped again. Tiny pieces of paper fluttered to the floor. And then Maddy's heart fluttered, too. She had an idea.

"Would you like to join in our fundraiser? You, me, and Darcy! We'll be a great team!"

Supply Closet
Strategizing

After Amina went home, Maddy climbed on her bed. She flopped onto her back. She had to come up with her present fund-raiser.

Her last project, the movie theater, had been tricky. But it had done really well. Maddy had worked hard.

After she saved the block party, her neighbors had given her a card. It said, *You're a top-notch CEO!* She kept it pinned to her bulletin board. She looked over at it now.

But what would she be the CEO of this time?

She started to clean up her wrapping paper, but then stopped. If Mom really wanted Maddy to wrap presents, there wasn't much point in cleaning yet.

Maybe Dad needed help wrapping, too. Hey, maybe they'd give her an extra allowance for helping!

She froze.

That's it! She could charge money to wrap people's holiday presents!

Most grown-ups didn't like to wrap presents. And even if they did, they didn't have the time. Everyone was busy, busy, busy this time of year.

Why not make money doing something she enjoyed? Something people desperately needed?

Maddy laughed out loud. She threw her snowmen cutouts up into the air. They floated back down on her.

The next day, Darcy didn't walk to school with Maddy. She had a dentist appointment. Maddy had to wait until right before lunch to tell Darcy.

The girls had volunteered to help their teacher. They were getting paper and paint from the supply room.

It was fun to have this responsibility. They giggled and skipped down the hall toward the stairs.

"Guess what?" said Maddy. "I'm going to start a new business!"

"Oh, yay!" Darcy stopped to jump up and down and clap her hands. "What is it? Can I help again?"

"Of course you can," said Maddy. The door to the dusty, cavernous supply room clanged shut behind them. "You have to! I think this time you should be . . . vice president!"

Maddy stopped and put her hand on Darcy's arm. "Oh, I forgot to tell you! I met a new girl, Amina. And she's going to help us."

Maddy told Darcy all about Amina, then scrunched up her face. "Is that okay with you? I mean, I know we're sort of partners. But she's nice, and she's really good at crafts."

"Totally!" said Darcy. "She can even be co-vice president with me! This way we can raise even more money. And buy really, really, really good presents for the teachers!"

Maddy smiled. "Now," she said, "time to strategize. Where are we going to have the wrapping stand? Or whatever we're going to call it?"

"Well," said Darcy, "last week we were at this department store. There was a table where people were wrapping presents. They were raising money for the animal shelter."

"Hmm," said Maddy. She leaned against a floor-to-ceiling shelf of colored construction paper.

"That could work. Or . . . I have another idea! Next Saturday is the Parkview neighborhood holiday fair. My parents were talking about it. We can totally set up a booth there!"

"Perfect!" said Darcy. "So where are we going to get wrapping stuff?"

She grabbed some glue sticks and construction paper. They were making paper mosaic picture frames in class. "I wish we had a supply room like this."

"I know," said Maddy. She looked around. It was a crafter's paradise. But these supplies were only for their school.

"Wait!" said Maddy. "There is a place like this we could go to!"

Whenever Mom decided their house was too jam-packed, she went on a clutter clearing rampage. Maddy and Drew usually tagged along to drop off the boxes. They'd take everything to a place called Scrap.

Scrap was like a thrift store, but for crafting items. It had all kinds of other random stuff. You could donate old bits of fabric, half-used notebooks, buttons, sea glass, candles, broken crayons, anything.

Scrap then organized the materials and gave them away for free. They prided themselves on keeping used items out of the landfill.

Maddy and Drew always came home with a few treasures.

"Scrap!" Maddy said to Darcy. "Oh, we just *have* to go! I'll ask Mom if she can bring us today after school."

Chapter Four

Mom couldn't bring them to Scrap.

"I have to pick up Drew at Will's house. Then stop at the store on the way home." It was after school. Mom, Maddy, and Darcy walked toward home. "What about tomorrow?"

"I guess," said Maddy. "Tomorrow will be okay."

As they arrived at the corner of Maddy's block, she paused.

"Maybe it's time for a business meeting," Maddy said.

Darcy looked where Maddy was gesturing. "Pie Place?" she asked.

"Please, Mom?" said Maddy, scrunching up her face.

Mom smiled. "Sure, why not."

Mom continued up the street toward home. And Darcy headed toward the Pie Place. Maddy hesitated.

"Darcy, wait!" she said.

Maddy had told Amina that she could be part of the team. It wouldn't be fair to have a meeting without her.

"Um, is it okay if we invite Amina?" she asked hesitantly. Maddy hoped that Darcy and Amina would like each other. Mixing friends could sometimes be hard.

The girls ran up the block to a purple house. It had a festive menorah in the window. Amina answered the bell.

When Maddy invited her to the meeting, a huge grin lit up Amina's face. Maddy knew it had been the right thing to do.

As the girls walked down the street, Maddy introduced them. She felt like a kid pretending to be a grown-up. "Um, this is Darcy. This is Amina," she said, rolling her eyes goofily.

Darcy and Amina took over from there.

"Guess what?" said Amina, as they turned the corner. "My mother enrolled me at your school. And I'll be starting tomorrow!"

Maddy nodded in approval. Now it made even more sense for Amina to be on their team.

The girls pushed open the Pie Place door. The bell on the door jingled.

Perfect for Christmastime, thought Maddy happily.

They ordered hot chocolates with homemade whipped cream. Then they settled into a table by the window.

"Feliz Navidad" was playing. Maddy hummed along as she pulled out her notebook.

"Okay, let's do the math part," she said. "If we wrap, I don't know, maybe twenty-five presents, and we charge $2 each, that's $50."

"Is that a lot?" asked Amina. "I'm not used to American money yet."

"Sounds like a lot to me," said Darcy. "I don't think we can charge more than that. No one will want to pay it."

Maddy took a sip of her drink and got whipped cream all over her mouth. She licked it off. "So instead," she said, "we need to get more customers."

"How?" asked Darcy.

"Marketing," said Maddy.

Amina nodded and looked thoughtful. Darcy looked confused. "What's marketing again?"

"It's sort of like advertising," said Maddy. "Making sure everyone knows about our business. Remember, for our movie theater we put up posters."

"Oh right." Darcy pointed. "Look. We could put our poster up there."

Maddy and Amina turned their heads toward the community board. It hung on the wall of the café. It was plastered with posters for babysitters, dog walkers, book readings, museum exhibits, and furniture for sale.

The girls contemplated the board.

"I don't think ours will stand out much," said Maddy. "Plus, only the people who come in here will see it.

We need to reach way more people than that!"

"Yeah. Remember when no one came to our first outdoor movie?" said Darcy.

"Oh, that was awful!" said Maddy, making a face. "Okay. How can we make sure everyone knows about our stand?"

Amina had been quiet for several minutes. But now she cleared her throat.

"I think I know what to do," said Amina. She put her finger in the air, pausing theatrically. "It's time to join the twenty-first century!"

"Yes!" said Darcy, and spilled her hot chocolate. "Whoops."

Chapter
Five

Request
Denied

Rasheed, the Pie Place owner, came to the rescue with a towel. "Big plans hatching?" He mopped up the spill.

Maddy blushed, but Darcy and Amina nodded emphatically. "Very big," said Amina. "Technology big."

Rasheed raised his eyebrows and finished wiping up.

Maddy frowned. She felt just a bit lost. It was time to catch up. "What do you mean?" she asked Amina. "How are we going to use technology?"

"We have to go high-tech," said Amina. "We have to use social media."

Maddy was up for anything if it helped them spread the word about their business. But she still didn't totally understand.

"Most refugees, like us, use social media," said Amina. "It helps us keep in touch with relatives back home.

"I can hear about Syria in the United States. I think we can spread the word about our business around a small neighborhood!"

Darcy was nodding. "I bet all the businesses do it," she said. "Ask Rasheed."

Maddy got up. She approached the counter. Rasheed looked up from the pie crust he was crimping.

"Professional query?" he asked.

Maddy tried not to blush again. "I was wondering. How did you tell people about your pop-up pie sale?"

"Your friend is on the right track," said Rasheed. He gave the pie crust a half turn. Maddy guessed he had overheard their conversation.

"You've got to use social media. There is an online neighborhood message group. Hundreds of people are members, all local. All you have to do is join it, then you can post a message."

"Thanks!" said Maddy, spinning back to her friends.

"And Maddy," said Rasheed. "Here's a piece of pie to split, on the house." He held out a plate with a slice of apple tart, drizzled with chocolate.

"Yum! Thanks again!" Maddy carried the slice back to Darcy and Amina. As they ate it, Maddy told them what Rasheed had said.

"Amina was right! Let's go back to my house and use the computer."

The girls carried their mugs up to the counter. Amina paused, confused, in front of the recycling and compost bins.

"Your plastic spoon goes in here." Maddy dropped hers in the blue bin. "Your napkin goes in the compost, the green bin."

"Maddy's really into being green." Darcy grinned at Amina. They waved to Rasheed and opened the glass door.

"Well, everyone should be," said Maddy, feeling defensive. "It's not like I'm a weirdo or something."

The door shut behind them, bell jingling.

"I know," said Darcy. "I didn't mean it like that." She took Maddy's hand. "I do all that stuff too. But what I really like is upcycling."

Amina listened, her forehead creased in interest.

"Oh, I love upcycling!" said Maddy. They turned the corner and headed up the street.

"I know, it's so cool. You use old stuff to make something new!" Darcy turned to Amina. "In third grade, we made wind chimes from old CDs."

"That's what Scrap is all about. I was excited about getting supplies there because it's free. We're also saving things from getting thrown out."

It was only 5:00 p.m. But it was already almost dark. Maddy pulled her coat tighter around herself.

The girls pointed out holiday decorations as they walked.

The Sanchez family had an inflatable snow globe. It had a wintry scene inside. The Larsons had strung their entire house with lights.

At the Kim house, they waved to Linus and Oliver. The boys were taping paper snowflakes to the front window.

The neighbors across the street had just pulled up. They had a tree on top of their car. Maddy's chest tightened like she might cry. In a good way.

They passed the Wolf house. Three candles on a menorah in the window shone bright. Amina popped in to tell her mom where she'd be. She joined the girls as they continued walking.

They walked up Maddy's front steps.
The lights in the tree outside turned on.
Maddy knew Dad had set the lights on
a timer, and it was just a coincidence.
But it still felt like magic.

They stepped inside. Maddy stopped to inhale the scent of fresh pine. Then she dashed into the living room.

"Mom, can I use the computer?" Maddy grabbed the laptop off of the desk.

"Maddy, you could at least say hi," said Mom. She came in, wiping her hands on a towel.

"Sorry! Hi, Mom," said Maddy, clutching the laptop. "We have to do some social media marketing!"

Mom said hello to Darcy and Amina. She asked Amina a few questions.

Maddy set up the laptop on the coffee table.

"Mom, we have to work!" said Maddy. She pulled Amina into the living room.

The girls grabbed a candy cane from the basket on the coffee table. They sat on the sofa, the computer in front of them.

"Okay, what do we do now?" Maddy asked.

Amina leaned forward and began clicking away. Maddy was a bit fuzzy on technology. Texting, emails, listservs, websites. The terms swam in her head.

But within a minute, Amina had located an online message group. It was for their neighborhood, Parkview. "It looks like anyone who lives, or has a business here, can join it."

Amina squinted to read some print. "All we have to do is send a request to join. Then someone will let us in, and we can post a message."

Maddy felt a little thrill. They had been so busy figuring out this social media thing. She'd briefly forgotten the whole reason they were doing this. The gift-wrapping business!

The girls sent a request to join. While they waited to be approved, they worked on their message.

"Start with something strong." Darcy wrestled with the plastic on her candy. "You do it, Maddy. You're a good writer."

"Okay, let me see." Maddy popped her candy cane in her mouth. She put her hands on the keyboard.

"How about this. 'Do you need more time?' No, wait. 'Running out of time? Let *us* wrap your presents! Come to our gift-wrapping booth during the holiday fair. This Saturday from 9 to 4.' "

"And don't forget to say it's for a good cause!" said Darcy.

Maddy would not forget that. She had learned from her mistake planning the block party fund-raiser. "Should we say it's to buy presents for the grown-ups at school?"

She removed her candy cane and examined it. She liked to suck it until it was a sharp point, no matter how tempting it was to crunch it. She put her hands back on the keyboard.

Darcy considered, adjusting a green plaid pillow behind her back. "Maybe that's too much," she said. "What about, 'Every penny for a good cause.' "

". . . good cause,' " repeated Maddy, typing. "Two dollars per present." She paused, then added, "All materials are recycled."

Amina read the ad aloud. "'Running out of time? Let *us* wrap your presents! Come to our gift-wrapping booth during the holiday fair. This Saturday from 9 to 4. Every penny for a good cause. All materials are recycled.' "

She hit some keys on the keyboard. "All materials are upcycled."

Maddy nodded. "Perfect."

"What if we still don't get enough customers?" Darcy asked. "I saw this cat castle that I want to get for Ms. Katey. She's always talking about her cats during library. But it's sort of expensive."

Maddy tugged on the plastic on her candy cane. Then she stuck it back in her mouth. She caught a glimpse of her sneakers.

"I know!" Maddy said. "If they get more presents wrapped, it costs less total."

Mom always brought her to the shoe store during their buy-one-get-the-second-half-off sale. "One present for two dollars, three presents for five dollars! That way they'll do more."

"Pretty good idea," said Darcy.

"I agree," said Amina, leaning in and adding the line.

And just then, they heard a ding. They looked at the computer. *Your request has been denied* read the message.

"What?" said Maddy. She cracked her candy cane with her teeth.

Chapter
Six

"Denied?" said Darcy, leaning over to take a closer look.

"Really?" asked Amina.

"They won't let us in the group!" Maddy paced around the room.

"That means we can't post our message!" she said. "And then no one will know about our booth. And we won't make any money. And we won't be able to buy any presents."

Maddy plopped down on the sofa again. She blew a big puff of air, and closed her eyes.

She'd thought they were almost done with this social media stuff. She wanted to get on to the fun parts. Like making the wrapping paper.

"You know who's also good at tech," said Mom. Mom was leaning against the doorway, arms crossed.

Maddy knew. "Drew?"

"Maybe it's time to delegate again," said Mom. "You need some advice. Drew could help. Ask him."

"Okay," said Maddy, nodding her head slowly.

"Plus," said Mom, "he's been a little bored lately. This will give him something to do."

Maddy found Drew in his room, reading an old superhero comic.

"Wait," he said. "You mean I could be in charge of handling your website? I'd get to send out updates and post messages?" He sat up straight and tossed the comic aside.

"Well, we don't have a website. And I'm not sure about updates," said

Maddy. "But yeah, maybe some of that stuff."

"Okay, I'll totally do it!" Drew said. He sprinted out of the room.

Drew squeezed in between Darcy and Amina. Amina pointed to the message. *Your request has been denied.*

Drew leaned over the laptop, typing and clicking.

"Okay, I think I see what you did wrong. See this form? You were supposed to explain why you wanted to join. They won't allow just anyone because you could be, like, a spammer.

You know, someone who joins groups and sends messages to ask for money."

Amina re-sent the request. This time, Maddy dictated a line. "We live on Twelfth Avenue. We'll be having a booth at the holiday fair on Saturday."

Five minutes later, they were in.

"Okay, let's post our message," said Maddy.

Darcy read it aloud. And then, *click*, *click*, *click*, Amina posted it.

"Yay!" said Maddy. "I wonder how long it'll take till people see it?"

It didn't take long.

"Hey, I got it!" called Mom. The kids raced into the kitchen. They found Mom looking at her phone. "See, I got the email with your message."

Maddy couldn't believe it. The words they had just typed, in this house, were being read by people all over the neighborhood! Social media was more fun, and useful, than she'd thought.

"Okay," said Drew, walking in circles. "What do you need me to do next? Want me to send follow-ups and reminders? Maybe three per day?

"There's this setting where people will see fireworks when they open a message! Maybe there's a Christmas carol app. That would be cool! What about setting up a Chirp account?"

Maddy caught Mom's eye and gave her a tiny smile. Drew certainly wasn't bored anymore.

Chapter Seven

On Tuesday, Mom fast-walked to school. Maddy, Amina, and Darcy trailed behind her, talking. Maddy and Darcy had been doing this for years. It was even more fun with Amina.

All day, Maddy could barely concentrate. They were going to Scrap after school!

Finally, the clock clicked 2:40 p.m. and the bell rang. Maddy and Darcy dashed out of the building to find Amina. Her classroom was on the other side of the school.

All three girls ran to the pickup line to wait for Maddy's mom. They piled in the car. "Seat belts, girls!"

Mom pulled out into the street and headed for Scrap. During the car ride, the girls planned what they'd need for the booth.

"Rolls of paper," said Maddy.

"Stamps," said Darcy. "And stamp pads. And hole punches. And ribbon. And paint!"

"Good thing we're driving," said Amina happily.

Mom sighed. "We might have to make two trips."

The girls laughed.

Scrap was located in what Mom called "the industrial part of town." They parked by a chain-link fence. Then they walked into the echoing warehouse.

A young woman with blue hair stood by the checkout counter. She greeted them. The girls looked in appreciation at the racks of wonderfulness.

"I'll be in the fabrics," said Mom.

Maddy grabbed some used paper shopping bags. She followed Darcy down the first cramped aisle. Amina walked next to her, eyes shining.

Maddy took in her surroundings. Office supplies of every kind. Binders, sheet protectors, staplers, file folders.

Art supplies galore. Paints, brushes, markers, colored pencils. Jars full of buttons. Bins of sea glass. Baskets.

Scraps of wood, picture frames, old CDs, miniature boxes left over from a company holiday party. A whole aisle of used toys. An entire room of holiday decorations. Maddy's chest swelled.

"Look what I found!" Darcy's voice jolted her back to reality. Darcy held an armful of half-used rolls of brown and white craft paper.

"Perfect!" said Maddy. She couldn't wait to decorate them.

Amina gasped. "Oh, I just had an idea! My grandmother makes the most wonderful embroidery decorations. I could do the same on paper! Can we find some needles and thread?"

They found that, and much, much more. When they met Mom at the register, they were so loaded down they could barely walk.

Maddy had bead garlands around her neck. Darcy was lugging a box of pine cones. And Amina's face was hidden among feather boas peeking out of her paper bag. She carried it with both arms.

Mom had an armload of fabrics, an antique clock, and a bike basket. "You never know what you'll find at Scrap!" She gave them an apologetic smile.

"Ready to check out?" asked the girl with blue hair. Although the items were free, the employees kept a careful inventory.

"We're ready!" said Darcy.

"So ready!" chimed in Amina from behind the feather boas.

Maddy bounced excitedly on her toes. She ducked her head to let the garlands drop onto the counter.

CHECK
OUT

77

Chapter Eight

Rain!

It was finally Saturday morning.

Rat-tat-tat-tat-tat. Maddy sat bolt upright in her bed. No, it couldn't be.

She ran to the window. Rain!

Not just drizzle, not just sprinkling, but pounding rain. Fair-canceling rain. Plans-ruining rain.

She charged into the dining room. She threw open the computer and went to the website.

"Holiday Fair Canceled Due To Rain."

Oh no! She trudged into the kitchen. As usual, Dad was already awake. He was drinking coffee and reading the paper. He looked up as she entered.

"What's wrong, Mads?" he asked.

Maddy tried to answer but couldn't. Her face scrunched up and she gave a choked gasp. She just pointed at the window. She pressed her face, wet with tears, into his chest.

"Ah," said Dad. "Rain. So that means . . . no fair?" Maddy nodded and Dad set down his paper. "But people still need their gifts wrapped. Fair or no fair, right?"

Maddy shrugged. "I guess," she said, her voice muffled against his shirt.

Dad gently pried her away from him. "Just because the fair's canceled doesn't mean your booth has to be."

Maddy sniffed and sat up a little. "But where can I set it up?" She remembered something Darcy had said. Darcy had seen a gift-wrapping booth inside a department store.

There weren't any department stores in her neighborhood. But there was . . .

"The variety store!" she said, and sat up straight. "It's big, they have room. It's right in the middle of the neighborhood. Everyone passes it all the time."

Dad nodded.

Maddy heard a footstep in the hall. Mom walked into the kitchen, yawning. Maddy explained the situation.

Mom thought the variety store idea was great. "Go ahead and call them," she said, pouring her coffee.

Maddy sighed. It was so easy for Mom. She loved talking to people, even strangers. Darcy and Amina would be good at this, too, Maddy suspected. She felt a pit in her stomach. But she didn't see any way out.

"I guess CEOs sometimes have to do things they don't want to," she said.

They looked up the variety store website. It opened at 8:00 a.m.

At 8:01, Maddy sat next to the phone. She set her script right in front of her. It told her exactly what to say. She dialed the number.

"Um, yes, can I speak to a manager? Oh, okay, um, so I have a question for you," she began.

"Yes!" Maddy said five minutes later.

She pumped her fists and twirled in a circle. She stopped to sneak a pecan from the sticky buns Mom was putting in the oven. Then she went back to twirling.

The variety store's owner, June, was thrilled to have Maddy's booth. June had been worried about the rain. Having Maddy would be just the incentive people needed to shop.

"But guess what!" said Maddy. "June said we could have another incentive. She'll give customers 10 percent off their purchase. They just need to pay to have it gift wrapped! That will get even more people to come!"

"Really?" said Mom, her eyes wide over her coffee cup. "That's amazing! See what happens when you just talk to people?"

"But how do I tell people about it?" asked Maddy.

Dad nodded. "If a sale happens at the variety store, and no shoppers are there, did it happen at all?"

Mom rolled her eyes. "Go wake up Drew," she told Maddy. "He has a message to send out."

Chapter
nine

Drew sent out a message. Despite the fair being canceled, the gift-wrapping booth would carry on. Customers would have to go to the variety store.

"Mention the 10% off!" said Maddy.

"Maddy, you're glowing," said Mom.

Maddy smiled. It was exciting to collaborate with a grown-up business person. It made Maddy feel very . . . grown-up herself.

"Okay, I have to get my supplies." Maddy raced back to her room.

She came staggering downstairs with her arms full. Rolls of paper, boxes of pre-cut cards, bags of ribbon, already cut and curled.

The three girls had worked hard all week. And Amina's beautiful hand-embroidered cards were the best part of all.

Dad and Maddy pulled out in the car, windshield wipers swishing. "I'll bring you some sticky buns!" said Mom, waving.

Dad and Maddy picked up Darcy first. Then they headed back down the block. They stopped at the Wolf house. Maddy jumped out to ring the bell.

Amina stepped onto the stoop. She had a phone to her ear and was speaking in a foreign language. She held up a finger and gave an eye roll.

Maddy waited, wondering who she was talking to. Finally, Amina hung up and left the phone in the house. She ran down the steps with Maddy.

"I was talking to my grandparents." Amina gave a big sigh as they climbed into the car. "I miss them. They wish they could come here. Maybe soon. When we get enough money."

Maddy's throat felt tight. She wished she had a magic wand. She could wave it and give Amina money to bring her grandparents over.

They arrived at the variety store. June greeted them. She helped them set up on a folding table.

The booth started off with a bang! The customers flowed into the store. Maddy, Darcy, and Amina wrapped, taped, and tied.

By late afternoon, the pre-decorated wrapping paper ran out. Darcy used the last piece for an especially large present. It was a huge box containing a barbecue.

The customer felt bad about using so much paper. She poked two extra dollars into the money box.

"Good luck, girls," she said, lugging away her box.

A dad and two kids stepped up. They held books to be wrapped.

"What are we going to do?" whispered Amina.

Maddy nibbled her pinkie fingernail. *Roll with the punches*, she remembered Mom saying last summer. She peeked at the kids. What did kids love to do? Draw!

Maddy grabbed a blank roll of paper they'd brought but not decorated. She spread it out on the table.

"Here," she said and smiled at the two kids. "You can decorate your own paper! We have stamps, hole punches, markers . . . "

"And stencils!" put in Darcy. She pushed the supplies toward the kids.

"Not bad," the dad answered. "Art lesson and gift wrapping in one. Good business strategy."

The three girls looked at each other and giggled. Another obstacle, overcome!

At 3:00 p.m., Amina had to go home. Her mom needed help cooking.

"Stop by on your way home, alright?" she asked. "I want to know how much money we made! And then we can start planning what to buy the teachers."

"Okay," said Darcy, giving her a hug. Maddy waved as Amina left.

Maddy absently played with a leftover scrap of ribbon. Something tugged at the insides of her head.

Amina needed something. Help bringing her grandparents to the United States.

Did Maddy's teacher need a new pair of earrings, quite so much? Did the librarian really need a cat castle? Maybe they would prefer something homemade, like Maddy's family.

Could they use the money for something more meaningful? Maddy kept playing with the ribbon.

The clock on the wall ticked to 4:00 p.m. Time to close up shop.

But there was one important thing left to do. They had to count the money. Maddy dragged Darcy into the break room in the back.

Maddy did the math in a notebook. "We made $124," she said.

"Whoa!" said Darcy. "That's way more than we expected!"

"Darce," said Maddy. "What if we don't buy presents and give the money to Amina? She could buy plane tickets to bring her grandparents to America."

Maddy explained about Amina's grandparents. Darcy was on board.

"After all," said Darcy, "you're like the craftiest person I know. We can make super awesome presents for the teachers, for free!"

Maddy was already racing out of the break room. When they arrived at Amina's house, they were out of breath. The rain had stopped. The sky was a beautiful smoky gray.

Maddy rang the bell. And waited. Her heart pumped from the run, and from excitement.

Amina answered. "Hi!" she said with a big grin.

Maddy held out the money box. "We have $124," she said. "For you! To help bring your grandparents to America."

Amina didn't take the box. She looked confused.

"What about the teachers?"

"We thought this was more important," said Maddy. "We . . ." She trailed off. Why didn't Amina look happier? Maddy gulped and looked at Darcy.

Darcy jumped in. "We both have our grandparents nearby. It must be sad for yours to be so far."

Amina was quiet for a moment. Finally she put out her hand. "Okay," she said. "Thanks."

Maddy hesitated. "Do . . . do you still want to hang out tonight?"

But Amina was already closing the door. "No, I'm still helping my mom cook. Bye."

She pushed the door closed with a click.

Maddy felt sick. She was no longer glowing.

Chapter Ten

Mom clicked on the electric kettle and set out three cups. Usually, Maddy loved choosing the fancy teacup for her nightly tea with Mom.

But today, all she could think of was Amina. Her cold face. Her shutting the door on Maddy and Darcy.

Mom had been baking during the day. She set a powdered sugar-dusted pecan crescent in front of each girl.

A tear ran down Maddy's face. It fell on her cookie with a plop. Despite her despair, a hiccupy-y laugh escaped her mouth. It turned into a sob.

"Oh, Maddy," said Mom. "Explain again why you think Amina is mad."

"She wasn't happy that we gave her the money."

Darcy agreed. "Yeah, she practically shoved us out the door. When she heard we'd changed the plan, she got upset. You could tell."

Mom poured their tea. "Maybe she felt left out. That you had changed the plan without her. You know, she's really enjoyed being part of this. She's been unsettled for so long. I bet it was nice to fit in, for once."

"Yikes," said Darcy, stirring her tea. "I guess we should say we're sorry."

"Yeah, I'm afraid to say you probably should," said Mom.

Maddy's heart sunk. She couldn't imagine anything more awkward.

"What if she's still mad after we say we're sorry?" she asked.

"That could happen," said Mom. "But it's worth a try."

Maddy stared bleakly at her cookie. "I thought the rain was the biggest problem." She trailed her finger through some sugar on the counter. "But this is much more horrible."

Mom sometimes said Maddy was a people-pleaser. Maybe she was. Maddy didn't like it when people were unhappy with her. Especially when it wasn't her fault. Maybe this time it was.

"Okay." She forced herself to stand. She made one foot after the other walk toward the front door. And just as she reached it, the doorbell rang.

There stood Amina. Like Maddy's, her face was blotchy.

Maddy felt like throwing up. She didn't know what to say. Amina had come here to get more mad at her!

But Amina didn't yell. Instead, she took a breath and started to speak quietly.

"I'm sorry I was mean," she said. "I felt bad."

"Oh," said Maddy. "I meant to be nice."

"I know. The thing is . . ." said Amina. "I felt so happy when I thought we were raising money to buy presents. I felt like part of a group!

"I'm so used to being an outsider. And people are always trying to help us, and it's nice. But it just makes me feel so different, so . . ." She paused, her face red.

"I get it," said Darcy. "My grandma felt like that when she immigrated here. She told me stories about it."

And Maddy got it, too. For once, Amina had been a regular kid in America. And then Maddy had gone and messed it all up.

"I'm sorry," whispered Maddy. She felt the tears coming again.

"I felt a bit left out," said Amina, looking at her feet. "I loved doing something with you and Darcy. When I learned you'd changed the plan, I felt bad. But I know you did it just to be nice. I'm sorry I got mad.

"Could we . . ." continued Amina. "Could we still make presents for the teachers? I've never done that before. It sounds like so much fun."

"Of course!" said Darcy. "Have you seen Maddy's art supplies?"

"I have, in fact," laughed Amina. And she reached out and hugged Maddy.

An elephant-sized weight lifted off Maddy's chest. She felt almost like singing.

She'd wanted to do something nice for Amina. Turns out, the nicest thing was just including her.

But Amina was still talking. "And, the money is exactly what we need. My parents have been saving, and this will help! My mother was so glad."

Maddy smiled. "Oh, I'm so happy!"

"You are going to love my grandmother," said Amina. "She's even craftier than us! Wait till you see the jewelry that she makes."

Just then, the doorbell rang again.

"My goodness," said Mom. "What a night!" She opened the door, and a crowd of faces beamed at them. Candles burned. "Merry Christmas!"

Maddy gasped. "Carolers!"

Amina looked confused. "What are carolers?"

"They're going house-to-house singing holiday songs," said Mom. She waved at people she knew in the crowd. "Oh, there's Finn, and Paige! And Bea and Alma and Sylvan!"

The crowd burst out into "Silent Night." Mom turned to the girls. "Let's join them! They invited us, and I forgot."

"Let's go!" said Darcy, pulling on her coat.

Maddy hesitated. It could be fun. But she had been outgoing enough for one day. "I'll pass out the cookies," she said.

"I'll go!" said Amina.

"Yay!" said Darcy. "I'll teach you the words."

Mom, Darcy, and Amina joined the carolers. Their voices floated up the steps to where Maddy stood. Her mind was happy, her body tired, her heart full.

A GUIDE FOR KID ENTREPRENEURS
Part 3: Marketing

Marketing helps promote your business. It gets the word out and brings in customers. Here are some ideas.

- Flyers and posters. Pass them out or post in local businesses.

- Annoucement. Make one at your school's morning circle.

- Social media. With a trusted adult, post in an online neighborhood group or send out emails.

- Incentives. Offer discounts, such as "10% off for first-time customers" or "buy one, get the second half-off."

- Word of mouth. Tell your friends, provide good service, and let the word spread.

AUTHOR BIOGRAPHY

Like her character Maddy McGuire, Emma Bland Smith loves coming up with crazy schemes, and writing children's books is her favorite one yet. Her first book was the award-winning Journey: Based on the True Story of OR7, the Most Famous Wolf in the West. Emma also works as a librarian in San Francisco, where she lives with her husband and two kids. (She hopes her neighbors will recognize the setting of the Maddy McGuire series!) Visit emmabsmith.com to learn more about Emma and her other books.

ILLUSTRATOR BIOGRAPHY

Lissy is an illustrator with a passion and love for animation, visual development, and children's books. She was born and raised in the Dominican Republic before moving to the United States, where she studied illustration at the University of the Arts of Philadelphia. Her passion with illustration and animation truly began after watching Spirited Away. Since then, Hayao Miyazaki has been her biggest artistic influence, while making people smile with beautiful and inspiring images has been her main purpose as an artist. Lissy absolutely loves collecting art books of all kinds, stargazing, traveling, and learning about different languages and cultures.